KT-409-248

# ALICE in WONDERLAND

BONNEY PRESS

Published by Bonney Press,
an imprint of Hinkler Books Pty Ltd
45–55 Fairchild Street
Heatherton Victoria 3202 Australia
www.hinkler.com

BONNEY
PRESS

© Hinkler Books Pty Ltd 2019

Cover design: Jess Matthews
Illustrator: Agnès Ernoult
Text adapted by: Katie Hewat
Design: Paul Scott and Patricia Hodges
Editorial: Emily Murray
Prepress: Splitting Image

All rights reserved. No part of this publication may be reproduced,
stored in a retrieval system, or transmitted in any way or by any means,
electronic, mechanical, photocopying, recording or otherwise,
without the prior written permission of Hinkler Books Pty Ltd.

ISBN: 978 1 4889 1305 1

Printed and bound in China

# ALICE in WONDERLAND

Based on the original story by
## LEWIS CARROLL

It was a very hot day and Alice and her sister were sitting by the pond in the shade of a great oak tree. They had just finished a wonderful picnic of honey cakes and lemon cakes, banana bread and fruit scones, chocolate cookies and blueberry crumpets. Alice was very full and felt very sleepy indeed.

Just then, Alice saw a White Rabbit hurrying by the hedge, wearing a waistcoat and muttering to himself.

'Oh dear! Oh dear!' said the White Rabbit. 'I shall be late. Oh dear! Oh dear!'

The Rabbit took a watch from his waistcoat pocket, looked at the time, and hurried on. Alice was very curious, and got to her feet. She followed the Rabbit and was just in time to see him pop under the hedge and down a rabbit hole.

Oddly enough, Alice didn't think it at all peculiar to see a talking rabbit in a waistcoat so, without hesitation, she followed him into the hole and found herself dropping down into what seemed to be a very deep well. The sides of the well were covered with cupboards and bookshelves, maps and hanging pictures. Down, down, down she went, until suddenly her fall came to an end with a thump! She landed on a thick pile of sticks and dry leaves.

Alice watched the Rabbit vanish through a tiny door with a tiny lock. Beside the door sat a glass table with a tiny golden key on top.

She tried the key in the lock and it opened right up! Through the door, Alice saw the most spectacular garden she could ever imagine, full of flowers and fountains and wonderful creatures.

But how would she ever fit through that door? She tried squeezing through headfirst, then feetfirst, with no luck. She closed the door and locked it, feeling terribly disappointed and wishing she had eaten fewer cakes for lunch.

When Alice stood up, she was amazed to see there was now a small bottle on the glass table. The label said 'Drink me!'

Alice put the key down on the table. She checked that the bottle was not marked poison (this was a lesson she had learned the previous summer after swiping a glass of what she mistakenly thought was cordial from the kitchen), then quickly gulped down some of its contents.

'What a curious feeling,' said Alice. 'I feel as if I've shrunk!' In fact, she had. 'How nice,' she thought. 'Now I can get through the door and into the garden.'

Then she remembered she had left the key on the table. 'Oh bother!' she exclaimed. 'I'm so small I can't reach the key!'

Alice tried to scramble up one of the table legs but, about halfway up, she could go no higher and slid and slipped all the way back to the bottom.

She decided to try again and this time she was determined to make it. She backed up all the way to the door to give herself a run-up. 'I've got it this time!' she said, and she took off as fast as she could. When she reached the table leg, she was racing along and she took a giant leap. She was delighted as she soared through the air, until she managed to get tangled in her skirts, missed her hold on the leg, and landed on the floor in a heap.

Alice dusted herself off and gave it one more try, before she finally sat down on the floor and burst into tears.

Once she had cried herself out, Alice noticed a small cake under the table. The icing spelled 'Eat me!'

'Well, it has been a while since lunch,' Alice thought, and she gobbled it up. Immediately she began to grow. 'Curiouser and curiouser!' she said.

Now she could reach the key, which she placed in her pocket. But, once again, she was far too big to fit through the door.

Alice opened the door and looked through into the garden, feeling very sad. Then she noticed that the bottle on the floor still had some liquid in it, so she drank it.

She waited and waited, but nothing seemed to happen. Alice burst into tears again: giant tears that just wouldn't stop. The giant tears began making puddles on the floor, and soon those puddles joined together and turned into a flood.

When she finally stopped crying and looked around, she realised that the flood of tears was carrying her through the open door. She had shrunk after all!

Once she was through the door, Alice saw that her tears had created a giant lake, and that all sorts of creatures from the garden had fallen in.

As she swam, she made friends with a mouse, a dodo and a parrot, and together they found their way to the edge of the lake. They climbed out, exhausted and soaking wet.

'However will we get dry?' asked Alice, which set off a rather confusing argument between the other creatures.

'We must name all the kings and queens of England, from first to last then last to first!' said the mouse.

'Nonsense!' screeched the parrot. 'We must do it my way, as I am the oldest.' But when asked what 'his way' was, he really had no idea.

Then the dodo declared, 'We must have a Dodo Race! Line up behind me!' And that seemed to settle it.

After they raced for half an hour, the dodo stopped and said, 'The race is over!'

'But who won the race?' asked Alice.

'We all did, because we are all dry!' replied the dodo.

Alice giggled and thought they were all quite mad. Suddenly she saw the White Rabbit dash by, so she said goodbye and ran after him.

Alice followed the Rabbit all the way to a sweet little cottage in a clearing. The Rabbit saw her and, mistaking her for his maid, shouted, 'Girl, go upstairs and find my gloves! Hurry, hurry, there's no time to lose!'

Alice, being the kind and helpful girl she was, rushed into the cottage and ran upstairs to search for the gloves. She found a pair of white gloves lying on a bedside table.

Beside them was a little bottle filled with sparkling liquid. It looked so delicious that Alice just couldn't resist. She picked up the bottle and, completely forgetting to check the label this time, took a little sip. Before she had even put down the bottle, she was growing.

She grew and grew until she was completely squashed inside the tiny cottage, with one arm hanging out of the window and one leg stuck right up the chimney! It was most uncomfortable.

Alice heard the front door open and footsteps running up the stairs. The Rabbit burst into the room and saw Alice. Completely terrified, he turned and dashed back out, yelling for help.

Soon, Alice could hear that a group had gathered outside and were suggesting ways to remove the giant from the house.

'We could climb through the window,' said one voice.

'Or go down the chimney,' suggested another.

'We'll have to burn it down!' added a third voice.

Alice was horrified. She was about to scream when some small pebbles started flying in through the window. A few landed on her nose, stinging.

'Ouch!' she cried and as she did, a pebble flew straight into her mouth. Alice was surprised and delighted to find that it was a delicious cookie! She chewed it and swallowed it and she immediately began to shrink. She was tempted to snack on a few more of the tasty treats, but she was already very small.

Alice tiptoed down the stairs and tried to sneak away, but outside she found a very cranky White Rabbit along with an angry lizard and two grumpy guinea pigs waiting for her. They began to chase Alice, so she fled away into the forest.

Alice decided that it was much too risky being this small in such a strange land, so she started searching around for something to eat that might make her taller again. Soon she came across a tasty-looking mushroom. She walked around the mushroom from one side to the other. She thought about having a nibble, but her mother had always warned her that eating wild mushrooms could make very strange things happen. Finally, Alice stood on her toes and peeked over the edge.

Alice was very surprised to see a large blue caterpillar sitting on top. And the caterpillar seemed very surprised to see Alice.

'Who are you?' he asked.

'I'm not so sure anymore,' replied Alice. 'I knew who I was when I got up this morning, but I have changed ever so many times since then.'

Alice thought the caterpillar might be able to help with her problem, so she asked if he knew any way she could grow taller. The caterpillar explained that eating one side of the mushroom would make her grow taller, while the other would make her shorter.

Alice broke a piece off each side of the mushroom. She nibbled at one piece, which made her shrink, so she quickly took little bites from the other piece until she reached her usual height.

'What a relief!' she exclaimed. 'It was such a bother being so small.'

The caterpillar looked at Alice disapprovingly. 'Of course you'll always be unhappy if you go around changing shapes and sizes all the time.'

Alice thought the caterpillar quite rude, so she turned and walked away.

'Let's see how you feel when you turn into a butterfly!' she mumbled under her breath as she left.

After a while, Alice sat down against a tree trunk to rest. She was startled to hear a voice. 'Hello there,' it said. Alice looked up and saw a huge cat hanging from one of the tree branches, grinning.

'Why are you grinning?' asked Alice.

'Because I am a Cheshire Cat,' it replied.

The cat's grin grew a little wider. Alice decided it must be friendly, so she asked, 'Would you please tell me which way I ought to go from here?'

'That depends on where you want to get to,' answered the Cat.

'I don't much care,' said Alice.

'Then,' purred the Cat, 'it doesn't really matter which way you go.'

Miraculously, as the Cat spoke, Alice saw its tail disappearing, followed by its body and then its face. Finally, only the grin remained. 'To the right lives the Hatter,' continued the Cat, 'and to the left lives the March Hare.'

The Cat grinned at Alice again and its body reappeared. 'You can go and visit either of them if you like, but they are both mad.'

'Everybody here is mad,' murmured Alice. She decided to head left.

After a long walk, she came upon a small house with two chimneys shaped like a hare's ears. Outside, at a large table, sat the March Hare and a very peculiar-looking fellow wearing a large top hat. The Hare looked up and saw Alice approaching. 'No room, no room!' he began shouting.

'How rude!' said Alice. 'There is plenty of room.' She sat down in a chair of her choosing.

'Have some wine!' said the Hatter. Alice thought this odd, since they were clearly having a tea party.

'I can't see any wine,' she said.

'Oh, there isn't any; only tea,' replied the Hatter.

Alice decided there was no point arguing, so instead she asked: 'Do you know the time?'

'Time?' said the Hatter. 'Do you know him too? I once had to sing a song about Time for the Queen of Hearts. During the first verse, she shouted, 'You're murdering Time! Off with your head!''

'How savage!' cried Alice.

'Oh, she wants to chop everyone's heads off. You'll see,' replied the Hatter as he picked up thc tcapot and splashed some tea on the dormouse's nose. The dormouse squealed and jumped out of the sugar bowl.

'Oh, you're awake!' said the March Hare to the dormouse. 'Tell us a story!'

'OK,' said the dormouse. It rubbed its nose and began: 'There were once three sisters who lived in a treacle well.'

'There's no such thing as a treacle well,' interrupted Alice. 'What nonsense!'

'If you think it's nonsense, maybe you should just be quiet!' said the Hatter.

Alice had never met anyone so rude, or quite so mad, in her life. 'That was the silliest tea party I have ever been to in my life,' she said to herself, and walked on.

As she walked, Alice noticed that one of the trees she was passing had a door leading right into it. When she opened it and went through, she found she was in the beautiful garden she had first seen when she went down the rabbit hole.

'Curiouser and curiouser!' she thought. 'But then everything today has been very curious.'

The garden was very lovely indeed. It was filled with the most colourful flowerbeds, and sprays of cool water flowed from fountains all over the garden.

There were gardeners everywhere, but to Alice's great surprise, they were all flat, rectangular playing cards. Each had a spade symbol on its front.

She walked over to the nearest group of gardeners, who, oddly enough, were painting a bush full of white roses red.

'Excuse me,' said Alice. 'May I ask why you are painting these roses red?'

'Because otherwise, it's off with our heads!' cried the Seven of Spades. The Five of Spades explained that they had accidentally planted white roses and the Queen of Hearts would be very angry.

Just then a trumpet sounded. The Spades fell flat to the ground, shaking terribly. Alice looked up to see a procession enter the garden, led by the King and Queen of Hearts. The Queen stopped when she saw what the gardeners had been doing and flew into a rage.

'Off with their heads!' she shouted, and a group of Clubs ran forward and dragged the gardeners away.

'Wait!' cried Alice. 'You can't do that!'

The Queen spun around, noticing Alice for the first time. 'Nobody tells me what to do in Wonderland!' she screeched. 'Off with your head!'

Just as the Clubs were about to grab hold of Alice, the King spoke quietly. 'Now, now dear, let's not spoil such a lovely day. Maybe the girl could join our game of croquet?'

The Queen nodded and moved on. The King whispered in Alice's ear, 'Not to worry, my dear: every time the Queen orders a beheading, I have the poor creature released as soon as they're out of sight.'

He gestured for Alice to join the procession.

They soon reached a field covered with ridges and ditches and the Queen called for the game to start. It was not like any game of croquet Alice had ever seen.

The Clubs spread themselves around the field and bent over backwards to form croquet hoops. The Six of Hearts handed each player a pink flamingo, which they were to hold upside-down to use as a croquet mallet. Then a group of hedgehogs waddled onto the field. One rolled up on the ground in front of each player to be used as a croquet ball!

When the game finally started, everybody played at the same time. Hedgehogs rolled into ditches and rolled up ridges to fly up in the air. Every few seconds Alice could hear the Queen shout, 'Off with his head!'

Alice feared the Queen's anger, so she was doing her very best to play, but with little success. Her flamingo kept twisting its head around no matter how politely she asked it to stay stiff, which made the other flamingos panic; and the hedgehogs were getting tired of being whacked around and so were trying their best to get off the field.

The game finally ended when the King and Alice were the only remaining players whose heads the Queen had not ordered off.

Alice had just flopped down on a grassy hill, quite exhausted, when she was approached by a griffin. He was an odd creature with the wings and head of an eagle and the body and tail of a lion.

'You must come with me!' the Griffin said. 'The Queen has ordered that you be taken to meet the Mock Turtle.'

Alice got up and followed. 'Whatever is a Mock Turtle?' she asked the Griffin, who looked at her as if she was quite peculiar.

'Why, it's what they use to make Mock Turtle soup, of course!' he replied.

Soon the pair came upon a rock, on top of which sat a curious creature who was part calf and part turtle, crying. Alice felt terrible for the poor sad creature and asked him what was wrong.

'I used to be a real turtle,' he said through his sobs. 'I used to swim in the ocean and go to a school. Our teacher was a wonderful old turtle we all called Tortoise.'

'Why did you call him Tortoise if he was a turtle?' asked Alice.

'Because he taught us, of course!' replied the Turtle. This made Alice giggle.

'I go to school too,' she said. 'I take lessons in French and music and lots of other things.'

'I used to take lessons in French, music, ambition, uglification and washing clothes,' the Griffin chimed in.

Alice didn't know what to say to that, so she turned back to the Mock Turtle. 'How long did you spend at school?' she asked.

'Ten hours on the first day, nine on the second, and so on,' he replied.

'How very odd!' said Alice.

'Well, that is the reason they're called lessons,' said the Griffin. 'Because they lessen by an hour each day.'

Alice was still laughing at this when she heard the White Rabbit's voice carry across the meadow: 'Hear ye! Hear ye! The trial is about to begin!'

'Come on!' cried the Griffin, and he took Alice by the hand and hurried off.

The Griffin dragged Alice along to the courthouse, where the King and Queen of Hearts sat on their thrones on a raised platform. The courtroom was full of every creature imaginable – in fact, it seemed like the whole of Wonderland was present.

The jury was made up of twelve creatures, a few of whom were familiar to Alice, including the angry lizard and the two grumpy guinea pigs from the Rabbit's cottage.

In the centre of the room was a table upon which sat many jam tarts.

They smelled delicious. Alice was wondering if it would be rude to take a tart when the doors burst open and two Clubs dragged in the Knave of Hearts.

'White Rabbit, read the charges,' said the King. The White Rabbit unrolled a scroll, cleared his throat and began:

'The Queen of Hearts, she made some tarts,

All on a summer day.

The Knave of Hearts, he stole those tarts,

And took them quite away.'

The crowd gasped. This was indeed a serious charge!

Soon Alice found herself in the midst of a very bizarre trial. The Queen demanded that the jury begin the trial by deciding whether the Knave was guilty, but the Rabbit insisted on hearing from the witnesses first.

He called the first witness: the Hatter. 'Well,' the Hatter began, waving his teacup as he spoke, 'The March Hare was ...'

'No I wasn't!' shouted the March Hare, leaping out of his seat before the Hatter could finish his sentence.

'Off with their heads!' shouted the Queen, and both the Hatter and the Hare were dragged away. 'Call the next witness!'

Alice was shocked when the White Rabbit turned to her and said, 'We call the girl.'

'What do you know of this crime?' asked the King.

'Why, nothing at all,' replied Alice.

'Liar!' shouted the Queen. 'Off with her head!'

Alice found herself growing quite angry. She'd had enough of this horrible queen. 'I'm not afraid of you!' she shouted. 'You're not even a real queen. You're all just a bunch of playing cards!'

As soon as those words left her lips, the Queen, the King and the guards all turned into normal playing cards. They flew into the air, fluttering all over the place. Alice put her hands above her head to protect herself and gave a little scream as the cards tumbled down ...

'Wake up! Wake up ... ' Alice heard a faint voice saying. She opened her eyes and saw some leaves fluttering down around her. She was back under the oak tree beside the pond.

'What a long sleep you've had,' said Alice's sister, who was sitting beside her.

Alice sat up and looked around, feeling very confused and a little hungry. 'I've had the most curious dream ... ' she said.